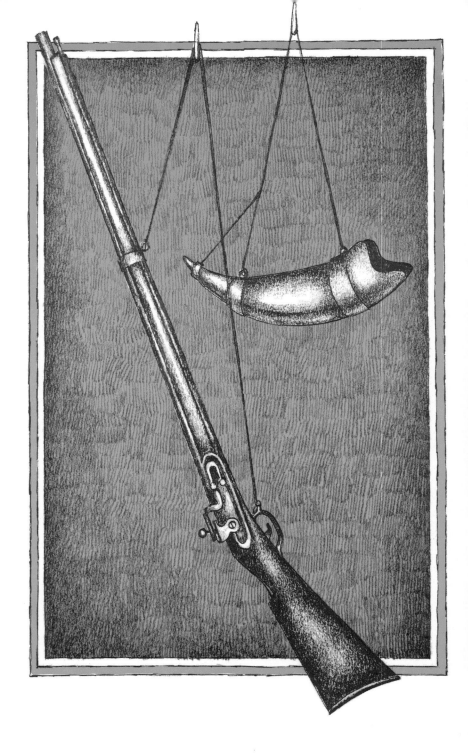

An I Can Read Book®

SAM
THE MINUTEMAN

BY NATHANIEL BENCHLEY
PICTURES BY ARNOLD LOBEL

HarperCollins*Publishers*

HarperCollins®, 🏠®, and I Can Read Book® are trademarks of HarperCollins Publishers Inc.

SAM THE MINUTEMAN
Text copyright © 1969 by Nathaniel G. Benchley
Pictures copyright © 1969 by Arnold Lobel

Library of Congress Catalog Card Number: 68-10211
ISBN 0-06-020479-6.–ISBN 0-06-020480-X (lib. bdg.)
ISBN 0-06-444107-5 (pbk.)
11 12 13 SCP 30 29 28

SAM THE MINUTEMAN

About two hundred years ago
a boy named Sam Brown
lived with his parents on a farm
in Lexington, Massachusetts,
near Boston.
At that time, America
was not a country of its own.
It belonged to England.

The farm was small,

and the earth was rocky.

Sam and his father did most
of the outdoor work together.

Sam's mother worked indoors.

Everything they needed,

they had to make

or grow

or cook

for themselves.

Once, in Boston,

Sam and his father saw the soldiers

the British King had sent

to keep order.

The people were unhappy

with the way things were being run.

Sometimes they had riots.

Some people hid guns and powder

in case of trouble with the soldiers.

They didn't like the soldiers much.

They called them Lobster Backs

because of their red coats.

On their way home,
Sam asked,
"What do these
soldiers want?"
"They want to keep us
from being too strong,"
his father said.
"They are afraid of us."
"That makes us even,"
said Sam.
"I'm afraid of them."

One night in early spring
Sam was awakened by the sound
of church bells ringing.
"What's this?"
he thought.
"It can't be
Sunday yet!"

He went to the window.

In the darkness

he could see men running.

They seemed to come from everywhere.

He heard the voices

of his father and his mother.

His mother sounded frightened.

Sam knew there was trouble.

He dressed quickly

and went downstairs.

"What's going on?" he asked.

"Go back to bed," his mother said.

"No," said his father.

"We need everyone we can get."

His father was a Minuteman,

which meant he had to be

ready for trouble

at a minute's notice.

"Get your gun, Sam," he said.

"Why?" asked Sam.

"What's happening?"

"Nobody knows for sure,"
his father said.

"The British have left Boston
and are coming this way."

"Who told you?" asked Sam,
hoping it wasn't true.

"Paul Revere," said his father.

"Now get your gun."

So Sam got his gun

and followed his father

through the darkness

to the village green.

The bells were still ringing,

and a drum was making

a rattling noise.

Sam felt cold and afraid.

27

Captain Parker,

the head of the Minutemen,

told them to line up

near the meeting house.

Sam saw his friend John Allen.

John looked the way Sam felt,

which made Sam feel better.

"Why are the British coming?"

Sam asked.

"They want the guns and powder

hidden in Concord," said John.

"They have to come past here

to get them."

Slowly, it began to get light.

The drums and the bells stopped.

It was so quiet

that Sam could hear the birds

twittering in the trees.

He could smell the apple blossoms

and feel the wet dew on the grass.

"Maybe they won't come, after all,"

he said to John.

"Maybe they'll go another way."

"Maybe," said John.

"But not likely."

Then it was daylight,

and the men began to relax.

Some of them even yawned.

Sam's father talked with friends.

Sam and John played games

with a knife in the grass.

Sam wished

he had eaten breakfast.

Suddenly John said,

"Listen!"

They listened,

and in the distance

they could hear

the sound of marching feet.

tramp tramp tramp

Tramp Tramp Tramp

TRAMP TRAMP TRAMP

TRAMP TRAMP TRAMP . . .

and THEN . . .

Over the hill

and past the tavern

came the soldiers!

They came on and on and on.

Sam could see their red coats

and the sun glinting

on their bayonets.

They looked like

a bright river of red.

As they came closer,

Captain Parker tried to count them.

There seemed to be a thousand.

And he had only eighty Minutemen.

"There are too many of them,"

he said.

"We had better move away."

"I'm all for that,"

said Sam.

"I think I'll get on home."

"Me too," said John.

"There's nothing I can do here."

Sam and John and their fathers
and the other Minutemen
began to move off.

"I'll see you after breakfast,"
Sam said to John.

Then he saw a British officer
who was shouting
and waving his sword.

"I wonder what he wants," Sam said.

"He told us to disperse," said John.

"I'm dispersing as fast as I can,"
said Sam.

"He doesn't need to shout."

Then someone, somewhere,

fired a gun—BANG!

The troops began to shoot.

Minutemen fell all around.

"Sam!" John cried. "I'm hit!"

John held his leg and fell down.

The British officer
made his troops stop shooting
and got them back in line.
He marched them off
toward Concord,
leaving eight dead Minutemen.

Sam and his father

helped John's father

take him home.

Sam felt he was having

a bad dream.

He saw John's mother crying

as she put a bandage

on his leg.

"How does it feel?" Sam asked.

"Not too good," said John.

When Sam and his father

got to their house,

all Sam's fear changed to anger.

"How did they dare do that?"

he cried.

"If they come back,

I'll shoot them—every one!"

"Be quiet," his father said,

washing the grit and powder

off his face.

"You may just have that chance."

"He will not,"

said his mother.

"He doesn't leave this house again."

Then the bells began to ring again!

The troops were coming back!

"Sam, you stay here!" said his mother.

But Sam had already grabbed his gun

and run outside.

His father followed close behind.

By now

more farmers had come

from all around.

They were shooting

at the soldiers

as they marched.

They never got in close

but fired from behind rocks

and trees.

This worked better

than meeting

in the open.

Then more British troops

came out from Boston.

For a while the battle was quite heavy

The British troops

burned some houses,

but their hearts weren't really in it.

Soon they headed back

to Boston,

followed on all sides

by the farmers,

whose bullets buzzed about like bees.

Late that night

Sam and his father got back home.

The rain was falling gently.

"Where have you been?"

Sam's mother said.

"I've been worried sick about you."

But Sam was too tired to answer.

All he wanted to do now was sleep.

No one knew it then,

but that day was the start

of the American Revolution.

The war lasted eight years.

At the end,

America was a country on its own.

But Sam didn't think of that.

He thought of John

and wondered how he was.

And then he slept.